W9-BHH-883

Love yourself
Help someone in need
include others
Give a compliment
Care for each other
Listen to each other
Cheer up a sad friend

Share

Thank someone

Care for animals

Bring flowers

to: George and the children

Forgive

Heather Lean

This book is given with love

To:

From:

Written by Heather Lean
Illustrated by Nino Aptsiauri
Edited by G. Nellist

 Published in the United States
by Puppy Dogs & Ice Cream, Inc.
ISBN: 978-1-955151-07-8
Edition: April 2021

For all inquiries, please contact us at:
info@puppysmiles.org

To see more of our books, visit us at:
www.PuppyDogsAndIceCream.com

Everything You Give Comes Back

Written By:
Heather Lean

Illustrated By:
Nino Aptsiauri

At dinnertime, the family shared their day.
Jordan barely listened, his mind was far away.

Later, in bed, he felt worried and sad.
"Oh, Mommy," he said, "my day was so bad.

People were cruel, and they said mean things, too.
I just didn't know what it was I should do."

"Oh, Jordan," said his mom. "What Grandma told me...
You must be the change that you want to see."

1

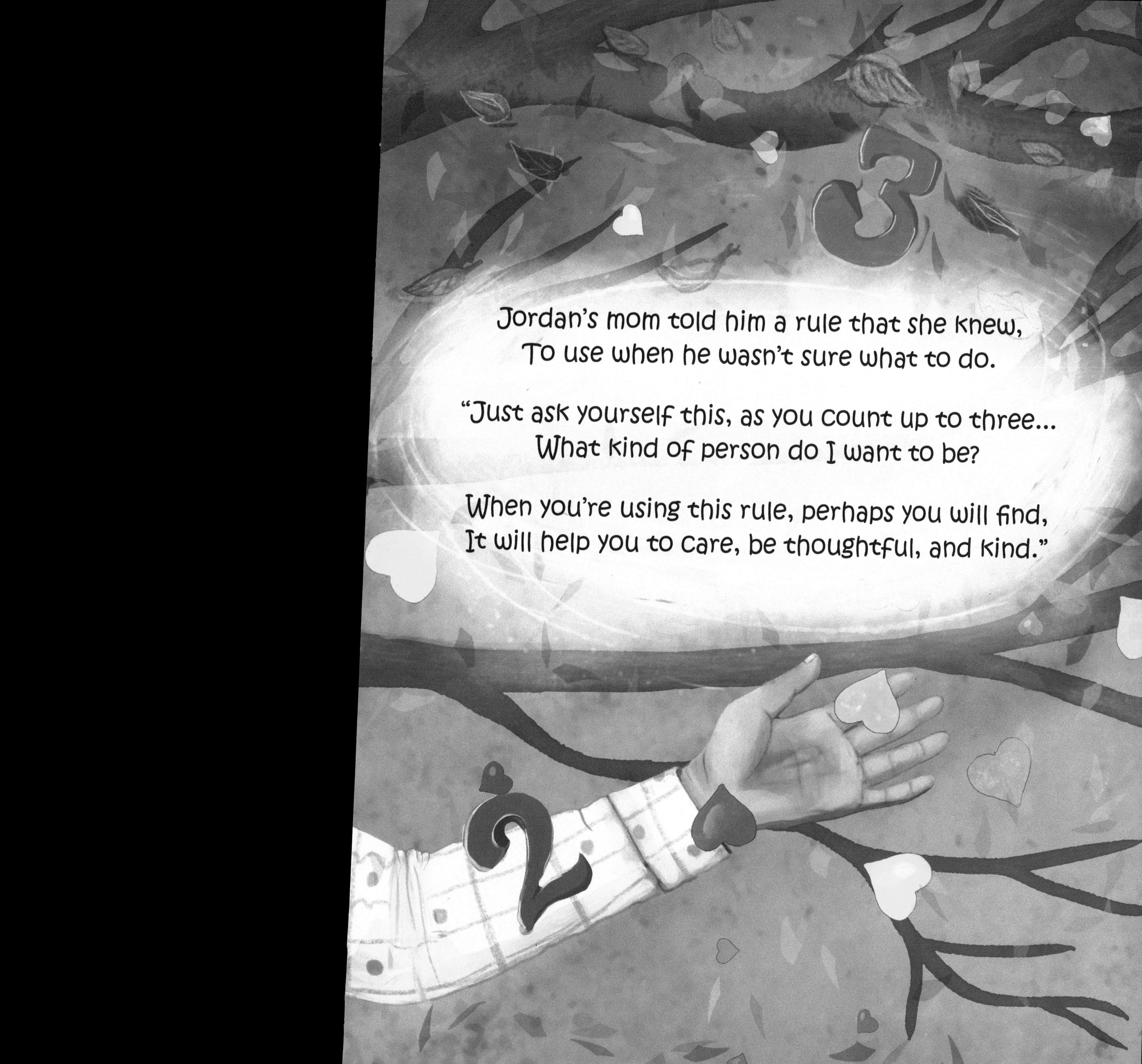

Jordan's mom told him a rule that she knew,
To use when he wasn't sure what to do.

"Just ask yourself this, as you count up to three...
What kind of person do I want to be?

When you're using this rule, perhaps you will find,
It will help you to care, be thoughtful, and kind."

The next day was much like the day before.
But Jordan was ready for what was in store.

When Sam, from his class, was hurt by someone,
Jordan thought back to the words from his mom...

“Close your eyes tight and just count up to three.
What kind of a person do you want to be?”

So Jordan reached out and stood at Sam’s side,
And gave him a hug and a grin super-wide!

It was lunchtime, and Jordan was just walking by
When he heard his friend, Faye, as she let out a sigh.

“I don’t have enough to buy that small snack.”
“Then I’ll buy it for you... and please don’t pay me back.”

Faye gave Jordan a kiss on the cheek.
“Oh, thank you!” she said, “That was really so sweet.”

The cashier then smiled, she’d seen the kind act,
And told Jordan something, a lovely life fact...

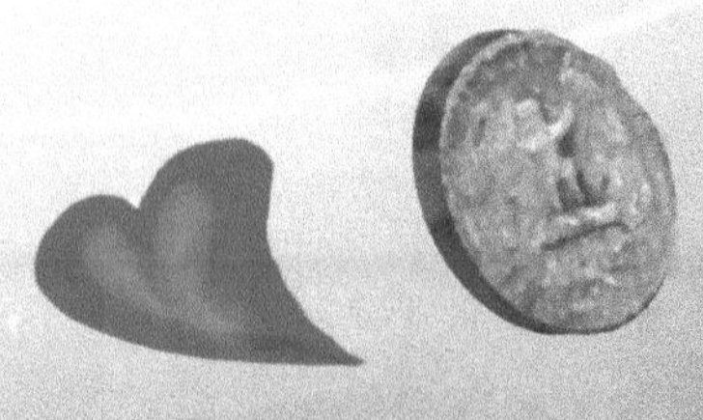

"Love travels around, around, and around.
When you get it, just give it, don't let it slow down.

There's no trick to it, no special knack,
For everything you give, it'll always come back."

At recess, the new girl, Livvy, was sad,
But Jordan knew just how to make her feel glad.
He went over and asked, "Did you want to play?"
And Livvy was thrilled – he'd just made her day!

Later, in Math class, Lance looked at his score.
He sighed and threw it down onto the floor.

But Jordan walked over to his frustrated buddy,
"Hey, Lance," he offered, "I can help you study!"

At her locker, Julie was brushing her hair.
She was lonely and just needed someone to care.

Jordan walked over and said, "Don't you see?
You're lovely just as you are... to me!

You don't have to look perfect, or be the very best.
Just be yourself, and you'll stand out from the rest!"

SCHOOL BUS
At the end of the day, as Jordan walked home,
He saw an old man who was walking alone,
"Please share my umbrella, it'll help keep you dry."
Oh, thank you," said the man, with a tear in his eye.

The rain had now stopped and it was sunny once more.
So on their way home, his family stopped at the store.

A woman was struggling in front of the shop
And had to pause as she let her heavy bags drop.

Jordan walked up and said, "Let me help you with those."
The woman was grateful for the kindness he showed.

CULINARY
30%
20%
10%

At home Jordan's grandma was out on her chair,
So he gathered some flowers to put in her hair.

"I love you Grandma," he said and kissed her face.
His grandma hugged him back with a warm embrace.

After dinner, with just one ice pop between two,
Jordan gave it to his sister, "This is for you."

"Oh, Jordan!" she smiled. "You're the absolute best!"
Then she broke it in half and they both shared the rest.

At bedtime Jordan's mom said with a smile,
"You remembered my words. I knew all the while.

Just how many lives have you touched today?
How many now know to give kindness away?

My sweet boy, this mom could not be more proud.
For love goes around, around, and around."

"Put your hand on your heart. Feel it beating right there?
Your heart is alive with love, hope, and care."

Then his mom leaned in and whispered, "It's true...
The love you give out comes right back to you."

Pay it Forward

Write the name and a kind deed you did for someone on the hearts below.

Name:

Kind Act:

Name:

Kind Act:

Name:

Kind Act:

Name:

Kind Act:

Claim Your FREE Gift!

Visit ➔ PDICBooks.com/Gift

Thank you for purchasing

"Everything You Give Comes Back,"

and welcome to the Puppy Dogs & Ice Cream family.

We're certain you're going to love the little gift
we've prepared for you at the website above.

Love yourself
Help someone in need
include others
Give a compliment
Care for each other
Listen to each other
Cheer up a sad friend

Share

Thank someone

Care for animals

Bring flowers

to: George and the children

Forgive

Heather Lean

CPSIA information can be obtained
at www.ICGtesting.com
Printed in the USA
BVHW060505011222
653162BV00028BA/601